To Maggie Kimbrall McCain,
for the healing power of her story.
And thanks to Bill Center,
my teacher, for his wisdom and kindness.
—B. R. M.

To my father.
—S. S.

The jeep grumbles and growls along the road. The top is rolled down, and the wind lifts the corner of my bandanna. Daddy and Mama are taking me to Grandmother's cabin way out in the woods by a lake. I will stay with her while Daddy and Mama find a home near Daddy's new job in Chicago.

When Daddy turns, the road becomes skinny like a snake. I lean back and close my eyes. I picture Grandmother in her blue cotton dress with the little flowers I can only see when I am close enough for a hug. Grandmother is Chippewa, like us. She is tiny and brown, with dark, shiny eyes that wrinkle in the corners when she smiles. She is almost light enough for me to lift in the air.

That is what I will do someday when I am a bigger girl. I will lift my grandmother into the sky. She will flutter and fly and sound like a bird when she laughs as we float above the trees.

The jeep stops. It is night outside. Grandmother opens
my door before I do, and I tumble toward her, half-asleep.
I lean against her as we walk to the cabin. The chilly night
wind races through the trees and around me.

In the copper pot on Grandmother's wood stove, water makes giggle sounds as it bubbles and boils. Heat pours from the stove, and soon my hands and face feel nice and warm.

The grownups start talking. I snuggle down on Grandmother's green couch and drift to sleep again.

This time, sleep is noisy and mean. Scary things that howl, whistle, and hoot like the night wind are so close! I scream and reach for Mama and Daddy, but in my dream they can't hear me. "Kimmy," Mama says as she holds me, "wake up! You're safe!" With Mama's arms around me, I am not afraid anymore. I feel her carry me to the bed in Grandmother's sewing room.

In the morning, sunshine is scattered over my bed and Grandmother's floor.

The grownups are talking in the kitchen. Mama's voice sounds different. I think maybe she is telling about my bad dreams.

I walk into the room and see Grandmother holding a small circle made of wood. Inside it is a web of leather string. Feathers are on top of the circle. Some hang down on a string with silver beads.

"Good morning," I say. "What's that?"

"A dreamcatcher," Grandmother says.

"What does it do?" I ask.

Grandmother laughs. "You'll find out."

The dreamcatcher's beads shimmer in the sunshine while I eat breakfast. When I see Daddy with a suitcase, I feel sad deep inside. Mama gets her coat, and I run to her.

"We'll only be gone a week," Mama says as they hug me goodbye.

I give them my tightest hugs. A week is too long!

Grandmother stands beside me. We watch the car grow smaller as they drive down the road. It's like another terrible dream just happened. I feel lost and alone.

"Come on, child," Grandmother says. "We have a dreamcatcher to make just for you."

In the woods by the lake, Grandmother and I find a green twig that bends. I find some black-and-white feathers.

Back inside the cabin, Grandmother brings beads, leather
string, and thin leather strips. She makes a circle out of the twig
and ties the ends together with a piece of leather.

I choose three silver beads and string them. Then I tie one
feather to the string. Grandmother loops a long piece of leather
string around and around inside the circle to make the web.
As she works, she tells me a story.

"Before you and I had grandmothers, a Chippewa girl had scary dreams," she says. "She would toss and turn and wake herself up with her own screams!"

"I do that," I say.

"So her grandmother did what our people still do. She asked the Great Spirit for help, and she was given a vision of a dreamcatcher circle. It had feathers on it just like yours and mine, but the inside was empty. When this grandmother hung the dreamcatcher above her grandchild's head, a spider came down and made the web inside. All the child's dreams were then caught in that web to go to the Great Spirit. Only the sweet dreams were permitted to go back to the girl."

"Did it work?" I ask.

"Of course," says Grandmother.

After we finish the dreamcatcher, we hang it above my pillow.

That night, I shiver when I think of Mama and Daddy so far away. Grandmother finds me. She sweeps back my hair as she rocks me. I am warm again.

Somehow, I am in my bed. I only remember my dreamcatcher floating above my head and Grandmother's hands as she tucks my blankets around me.

When I awake, I see my dreamcatcher turn in the morning light. Grandmother peeks in the room.

"I'm happy, Grandmother," I tell her. "My bad dreams didn't come last night!"

Grandmother's whole face crinkles around her smile.

We go to the kitchen. "Mama and Daddy will like my dreamcatcher," I say as Grandmother cooks crispy fry bread.

"I think so," says Grandmother. "In your new house, the dreamcatcher will be in your room."

"I miss them very much," I tell her.

Grandmother hugs me close. "Kimmy, Mama and Daddy will come for you," she says in her quiet voice. "Then you and I will surprise them!"

"How will we do that?" I ask.

"We will make presents for your new home," answers Grandmother.

Each night, I sleep under my dreamcatcher. My dreams are happy and peaceful.

Each day, Grandmother and I are busy with our work. We sew beads on leather to make hair ties for Mama. Grandmother takes me fishing, and I find a special feather just for Daddy. We make a dreamcatcher for Mama and Daddy.

But my favorite surprise is the picture I make of my family! There's Grandmother, Daddy, Mama, and me under my dreamcatcher. Rainbow colors splash out of the feather.

And when Mama and Daddy come back, that's the present they like best.

To Make Your Own Dreamcatcher

What you need:

- A grownup helper if you are not yet in fourth grade
- Scissors and all-purpose crafts glue
- A macramé ring 3 inches in diameter; available in crafts stores.
- Suede lace (2 yards) and sinew (synthetic or leather string) (3 yards); both are available in crafts stores.
- A clip or clothespin to hold suede lace in place after gluing
- A ruler
- Beads that you can string on the suede lace
- Several feathers

What to do:

Figure A:

Figure A

1. Cut a 5-foot piece of suede lace. Tie one end to the circle frame.
2. Wrap the lace around the frame to cover it, pulling tight as you go. Cut off any extra lace. Glue, then hold the lace end in place with the clip or clothespin while the glue sets.

Figure B:

Figure B

3. Cut a 1-yard piece of sinew. With one end, make a half-knot at the top of the circle.

Figure C:

Figure C

4. In a clockwise motion, make half-knots around the circle, about an inch apart. Continuing clockwise, keep using half-knots to make the rest of the web.

Figure D:

5. Gently tighten each half-knot in the center of your circle to make the middle hole of the web. Tie off the web with two knots. Cut off any extra sinew.
6. String beads on some of the remaining lace. Knot one end so the beads will not fall off. Tie the other end to the bottom of the dreamcatcher so the beads hang down.
7. Push the quill of the feather up through the bead holes. Or, with some leftover sinew, tie the feather to the beaded lace.
8. Tie the remaining feathers to the top of the dreamcatcher with some leftover sinew.
9. With the rest of the sinew, hang the dreamcatcher over your bed, away from the wall. It should hang above your head.
10. May you have sweet dreams!

Figure D

Someday you may wish to make a dreamcatcher using a twig, as Grandmother did. Soak the twig in water to make it bend into a circle without breaking. Then tie the ends together with sinew and proceed as above.

Grandmother's
Dreamcatcher

Becky Ray McCain

ILLUSTRATED BY Stacey Schuett

Albert Whitman & Company • Chicago, Illinois

Library of Congress Cataloging-in-Publication Data

McCain, Becky R. (Becky Ray)

Grandmother's dreamcatcher / by Becky Ray McCain; illustrated by Stacey Schuett.

p.   cm.

Summary: While spending a week with her grandmother who, like her, is a Chippewa Indian,

Kimmy learns to make a dreamcatcher, which allows the sleeper to have only sweet dreams.

ISBN O-8075-3031-X

[I. Grandmothers—Fiction. 2. Dreams—Fiction. 3. Ojibwa Indians—Fiction.

4. Indians of North America—Great Lakes Region—Fiction.] I. Schuett, Stacey, ill. II. Title.

PZ7.M4783375Gr   1998   [E]—dc21   98-4996

CIP   AC

Printed in China

10 9 BP 16 15 14 13

The paintings are rendered in acrylic and gouache on Rives BFK paper.

The design is by Scott Piehl.

Albert Whitman & Company is also the publisher of The Boxcar Children® Mysteries.

For more information about all our fine books, visit us at www.awhitmanco.com.